DON QUIXOTE

by Miguel de Cervantes

retold by James Baldwin

The Ingenious Gentleman, Don Quixote de la Mancha was originally written in Spanish by Miguel de Cervantes Saavedra. In its original form, it fills more than a thousand closely printed pages. It was published in two parts, the first in 1605 and the second in 1615. The novel was wildly popular in its time and has since been translated into many different languages. The story of the aging, idealistic, and overly imaginative knight has continued to influence readers, writers, and artists around the world. This edition offers a selection of famous episodes retold for young readers.

Adapted from *Don Quixote for Young People* by James Baldwin (New York: American Book Company, 1910).

Editor: John Holdren

Art Director: Steve Godwin

Designer: Jayoung Cho

Illustrators:
Jayoung Cho
G.A. Harker (from the 1910 *Don Quixote for Young People*)

ISBN: 1-931728-44-5

Printed by Worzalla, Stevens Point, WI, USA, April 2018

DON QUIXOTE

DON QUIXOTE

1. GETTING READY FOR ADVENTURES

Many years ago there lived in Spain a very old-fashioned gentleman you would have been glad to know. This gentleman had many odd ways and did many strange things. He not only amused his neighbors and distressed his friends, but also made himself famous throughout the world.

What his real name was, no one outside of his village seemed to know. Some said it was this, some said it was that. But his neighbors called him "the good Mr. Quixana," and no doubt this was correct.

He was gentle and kind, and very brave, and all who knew him loved him. He had neither wife nor child. He lived with his niece in his own farmhouse close by a quiet little village in the province of La Mancha.

His niece was not yet twenty years of age, so the house was kept and managed by an old servant woman who was more talkative than wise. A poor man who lived in a cottage nearby was employed to do the work on the farm. He did this work so well that the master had much leisure time and was little troubled with the cares of business.

Mr. Quixana was rather odd in his appearance and dress, as old-fashioned gentlemen are apt to be. He was more than fifty years of age, and quite tall and slender. His face was thin, his nose was long, and his hair was turning gray. He dressed very plainly. On weekdays he wore a coarse shirt and blue trousers of a homespun stuff. On Sundays, however, he put on a plush coat and short velvet breeches and soft slippers with silver buckles.

In the hallway of his old-fashioned house a short, rusty sword was always hanging. And leaning against the wall were a rusty lance and a big rawhide shield. These weapons had belonged to his great-grandfather long ago, when men knew but little about guns and gunpowder.

On the kitchen doorsteps an old greyhound was always lying asleep. This dog was very lean and slender, and his hunting days had long been past. In the barn there was a horse as old and as lean as the greyhound. But of this horse I will tell you much more in the course of my story.

Like many other old-fashioned gentlemen, Mr. Quixana did not work much. Rather, he spent almost all his time in reading, reading, reading.

He was seldom seen without a book in his hand. When the weather was fine he would sit in his little library, or under the apple trees in his garden, and read all day. Sometimes he sat up and read all night. He often forgot to come to his meals. He was so wrapped up in his books that he forgot his horse, his dog, and his niece. He forgot his friends, and he even forgot himself.

Now, what kind of books do you suppose he read? He read no histories or books of travel. He cared nothing for poetry or philosophy. His whole mind was given to stories of knights and their daring deeds.

He read so many of these stories that he could not think of anything else. His head was full of knights and knightly deeds of bravery and chivalry, of tournaments and battlefields, of wizardry and magical enchantments.

In general, much reading improves the mind. But because our gentleman read nothing but stories of knights and their adventures, he would have been wiser if he had read less.

At length this old-fashioned gentleman said to himself, "Why should I always be a plain farmer and sit here at home? Why may I not become a famous knight?" The more he thought about this matter, the more he wished to be a hero like those of whom he had read in his books.

"Yes, I will be a knight," he said to himself. "My mind is fully made up. I will arm myself in a suit of armor, I will mount my noble steed, and I will ride out into the world to seek adventures. No danger will frighten me. With my strong arm I will go forth to protect the weak and befriend the friendless. Yes, I will be a knight, and I will fight against injustice wherever I find it!"

So he began at once to get ready for his great undertaking. The first thing to be done was to find some suitable armor. For what knight ever rode out into the world without being encased in steel?

In the garret of his house there was an old suit of armor. It had lain there among the dust and cobwebs for a hundred years and more. It was rusted and battered, and some of the parts were missing. It was a poor piece of work at the very best.

But he cleaned it as well as he could, and polished it with great care. He cut some pieces of pasteboard to supply the missing parts, and painted them to look like steel. When they were properly fitted, they served the purpose, especially as long as no fighting was to be done.

With the suit of armor there was an old brass helmet. It, too, was broken, and the straps for holding it on were lost. But Mr. Quixana patched it up and found some green ribbons to use instead of straps. As he held it up and looked at it, he imagined how people would admire him when they saw his head in so rare a piece of workmanship.

And now a steed must be provided, for every knight must have a noble horse. The poor old creature in the barn was gaunt and thin and bony, but he was just the stuff for a war horse, wiry and very stubborn. As the old-fashioned gentleman looked at him, he fancied that no steed had ever been so beautiful or so swift.

"He will carry me most gallantly," he said, "and I shall be proud of him. But what shall I call him? A horse that is ridden by a noble knight must have an honorable and high-sounding name."

So he spent four days in studying what he should call his steed. At last he said, "I have it. His name shall be Rocinante."

"And why do you give him that strange name?" asked his niece.

"I will tell you," he answered. "The word *rocin* means 'common horse,' and the word *ante* is good Latin for 'before'

or 'formerly.' Now if I call my gallant steed 'Formerly-a-Common-Horse,' the meaning is plain, for everybody will understand that he is now no longer common, but very uncommon. Do you see? So, his name shall be Rocinante."

Then he patted the horse lovingly, and gently repeated "Rocinante! Rocinante!"

He thought that if he could only find as good a name for himself, he would feel like riding out and beginning his adventures at once. For what more could he need?

"Every knight," he said, "has the right to put *Don* at the beginning of his name, for that is a title of honor and respect. Now, I shall call myself Don—Don—Don something. But what shall it be?"

He puzzled over this question for eight days. Then a happy thought came into his mind.

"I will call myself Don Quixote," he cried. "And since my home is in the district of La Mancha, I shall be known throughout the world as Don Quixote de la Mancha. What name is more noble than that? What title can be more honorable?"

The good old gentleman had now mended and polished his armor and found new names for himself and his steed. He felt well equipped for adventures. But suddenly the thought came to him that he must settle still another matter before he could ride out and do battle as a real and true knight.

In all the stories he had read, every hero who was worthy of knighthood had claims to call out the name of some fair lady in time of peril. To her he brought the prizes he had won. To her he sent the enemies he had defeated to beg her forgiveness. It was at her feet that the knight must kneel at the end of every quest. It was from her that he must receive the victor's crown. To him, therefore, such a lady was as necessary as a steed or a suit of armor.

"After all," he thought, "I might come upon some evil giant—a thing that often happens to knights, as I have read. And if he and I should trade blows, and I should finally subdue him, then there must be a gracious lady to whom I might send him. Yes, he must fall upon his knees before my sweet lady and say, in a humble tone of voice, 'I, lady, am the giant Caraculiambro, who has been overcome in single combat by that most excellent of knights, Don Quixote de la Mancha. He has sent me to present myself before your ladyship, so that you may do with me as you will.'"

Don Quixote smiled as he imagined the scene. His smile, however, turned to a frown as he recalled that he was not acquainted with many ladies. Still, he felt that, as a knight, he must center his thoughts upon someone who would be his guiding star as he went faring through the world. And yet, who should it be?

This question troubled him more than any other. He sat in his house for two whole weeks, and thought of nothing else.

"Perhaps," he thought, "my niece would do?" After all, she was very young, and he was her uncle. But in all the books in his library, there was no account of a knight kneeling at the feet of his own niece. So, she would not do, no indeed, not at all.

At length he remembered a handsome, red-cheeked maiden who lived in or near the village of Toboso. Her name was Aldonza Lorenzo, and many years ago she had smiled at him as he was passing her on the road. He had not seen her since she had grown up, but he was certain that she must now be the most charming of womankind. He fancied that no lady in the world was better fitted to receive his knightly homage.

"Aldonza Lorenzo it shall be!" he cried, rubbing his hands together.

But what a name! How would it sound when spoken with that of the valorous Don Quixote de la Mancha? Surely it was too common, and she must have a title more like that of a princess. What should it be?

He studied over this for many days. At last he hit upon a name that pleased him very much.

"It shall be Dulcinea," he cried. "It shall be Dulcinea del Toboso. No other name is so sweet, so harmonious, so out of the ordinary, like the lady herself."

Thus, after weeks of labor and study, Don Quixote de la Mancha felt himself prepared to ride forth into the world to seek adventures. He waited only for a suitable opportunity to put his cherished plans into execution.

2. The Adventure at the Inn

One morning in midsummer, Don Quixote arose very early, long before anyone else was awake. He put on his suit of armor and the old helmet he had patched with pasteboard and green ribbons. He took down the short sword that had been his great-grandfather's and belted it to his side. He grasped his long lance. He swung the leather shield under his shoulder. Then he went out very quietly by the back door, so as not to waken his niece or the housekeeper.

He went softly to the barn and saddled his steed. Then he sallied forth through the back gate of the stable yard and rode silently away through the sleeping village and the quiet fields.

He was pleased to think how easily he had managed things. He was glad that he had gotten away from the house and the village without any unpleasant scenes.

"I trust that I shall presently meet with some worthy adventure," he said to himself. But soon a dreadful thought came into his mind: He was not a true knight, for no one had conferred that honor upon him. Surely the laws of chivalry would not permit him to do battle with anyone of noble rank until he himself was dubbed a knight.

"Whoa, Rocinante!" he said. "I must consider this matter." He stopped underneath a tree, and thought and thought. Must he give up his enterprise and return home?

"No, that I shall never do!" he cried. "I will ride onward, and the first worthy man that I meet shall make me knight, as often happens in the books I have read."

So he spoke cheeringly to Rocinante and resumed his journey. He dropped the reins loosely upon his horse's neck, and allowed him to stroll hither and thither as he pleased.

"It is thus," he said, "that my books say that knights ride out upon their quests. They go where fortune and their steeds may carry them."

Thus he sat leisurely in the saddle, while Rocinante wandered in little-traveled paths, cropped the green grass by the roadside, or rested in the shade of some friendly tree. The hours passed, but neither man nor beast noticed the time or distance.

"We shall have an adventure by and by," said Don Quixote softly to himself.

The sun was just sinking in the west when Rocinante, in quest of sweeter grass, carried his master to the summit of a gentle hill. There, in the valley below him, Don Quixote beheld a little inn nestled snugly by the roadside.

"Ha!" he cried. "Did I not say that we should have an adventure?"

He gathered up the reins, took his long lance in his hand, struck spurs into his loitering steed, and charged down the hill with the speed of a plow horse.

Because everything that Don Quixote thought came from the pages of the storybooks he had read, he imagined that the inn was a great castle with four towers and a deep moat and a drawbridge. At some distance from the gate he brought Rocinante to a halt and waited. He expected to see a dwarf come out on the wall of the castle and sound a trumpet to give notice of the arrival of a strange knight, for so it always happened in the books he had read.

But nobody came. Don Quixote grew impatient. At length he urged Rocinante forward at a gentle pace, and was soon within hailing distance of the inn. Just then a swineherd in a nearby field blew his horn to call his pigs together.

"Ah, ha!" cried Don Quixote. "There is the dwarf at last. He is blowing his bugle to tell them that I am coming." And with the greatest joy in the world he rode onward to the door of the inn.

The innkeeper was both fat and jolly. When he saw Don Quixote riding up, he went out to welcome him. He could not help being startled at the war-like appearance of his visitor, with his long lance, his battered shield, and his ancient coat of armor. But he kept as sober a face as possible and spoke very humbly.

"Sir Knight," he said, "will you honor me by alighting from your steed? I have no bed to offer you, but anything else you might want, you shall have in great abundance."

Don Quixote still supposed that the inn was a castle, and he took the innkeeper for the governor of the castle. He answered in lofty tones, "Señor Castellano, anything you may offer is enough for me. I care for nothing but arms, and no bed is so sweet to me as the field of battle."

G·A·HARKER·

The innkeeper was much amused. "You speak well, Sir Knight," he said. "Since your wants are so few, I can promise that you shall lack nothing. Alight, and enter!" And with that he went and held Don Quixote's stirrup while he dismounted.

The poor old man had eaten nothing all day. His armor was very heavy. He was stiff from riding so long. He could hardly stand on his feet. But with the innkeeper's help he was soon comfortably seated in the kitchen of the inn.

"I pray you, Señor Castellano," he said, "take good care of my steed. There is not a finer horse in the universe."

The innkeeper cast a doubtful glance at Rocinante, but promised that the horse should lack nothing, and led him away to the stable.

When he returned to the kitchen, he found Don Quixote pulling off his armor. He had removed most of it, but, as I have told you, the helmet had been tied fast with the green ribbons, and it could not be taken off without cutting them. But when a lady offered to help cut them, Don Quixote cried, "Never shall any one harm those ribbons!" And so, since he could not untie the ribbons, he had to sit there with his head enclosed in the old, patched-up helmet.

"Now, Sir Knight," said the innkeeper, "will you not partake of a little food? It is quite past our suppertime, and all our guests have eaten. But perhaps you will not object to taking a little refreshment alone."

"I will, indeed, take some with all my heart," answered Don Quixote. "I think I shall enjoy a few mouthfuls of food more than anything else in the world."

As ill luck would have it, there was no meat left in the house. There were only a few small pieces of salt fish in the pantry, and these had been picked over by the other guests.

"Will you try some of our fish?" asked the landlord. "They are very small, but they are wholesome."

"Well," answered Don Quixote, "if there are several of the small fry, I shall like them as well as a single large fish. But whatever you have, I pray you bring it quickly, for the heavy armor and the day's travel have given me a good appetite."

So a small table was set close by the door, for the sake of fresh air, and Don Quixote drew his chair up beside it. Then the innkeeper brought some bits of the poorly cooked fish, along with some bread as brown and moldy as Don Quixote's armor. As for drink, there was nothing but tepid water.

It was hard for the poor man to get the food to his mouth, for his helmet was much in his way. As for drinking anything, that seemed impossible. But then the innkeeper gave Don Quixote a hollow reed, through which he could sip the water. By using both hands, he managed to help himself and satisfy his appetite.

"No true knight will complain of that which is set before him," he said to himself. And indeed, he saw no reason to complain. For in his mind he saw himself in a scene from one of his beloved storybooks: He was a guest at a great castle, the fish was the finest trout, the bread was warm and fresh, and the water was a delicate wine.

Suddenly, however, the thought again came to him that he was not yet a knight. He stopped eating. The last poor morsel of fish was left untouched on the table before him. "Alas!" he groaned. "I cannot lawfully ride out on any adventure until I have been dubbed a knight. I must see to this business at once."

He arose and beckoned to the innkeeper to follow him to the barn. "Sir, I have something to say to you," he whispered.

"Your steed, Sir Knight," said the innkeeper, "has already had his oats. I assure you he will be well taken care of."

"It is not of the steed that I wish to speak," answered Don Quixote, and he carefully shut the door behind him.

Then falling at the innkeeper's feet, he cried, "Sir, I shall never rise from this place till you have promised to grant the boon which I am about to beg of you."

The innkeeper did not know what to do. He tried to raise the poor man up, but he could not. At last he said, "I promise. Name the boon which you wish, and I will give it to you."

"Oh, noble sir," answered Don Quixote, "I knew you would not refuse me. The boon which I beg is this: Allow me to watch my armor in the chapel of your castle tonight, and then in the morning—oh, in the morning—"

"And what shall I do in the morning?" asked the innkeeper.

"Kind sir," he answered, "do this: Bestow on me the honor of knighthood. For I long to ride through every corner of the earth in quest of adventures. But this I cannot do until after I have been dubbed a knight."

The innkeeper smiled, and his eyes twinkled, for he was a jolly fellow, and he saw here a chance for some merry sport. "Certainly, certainly," he said. "You are well worthy to be a knight, and I honor you for choosing so noble a calling. Arise, and I will do all that you ask of me."

"I thank you," said Don Quixote. "Now lead me to your chapel. I will watch my armor there, as many a true and worthy knight has done in the days of yore."

"I would gladly lead you there," said the innkeeper, "but at the present time there is no chapel in my castle. It will do just as well, however, to watch your armor in some other convenient place. Many of the greatest knights have done this when there was no chapel to be found."

"Noble sir, I believe you are right," said Don Quixote. "I have read of their doing so. And since you have no chapel, I shall be content with any place."

"Then bring your armor into the courtyard of my castle," said the innkeeper. "Guard it bravely until morning, and at sunrise I will dub you a knight."

"I thank you, noble sir," said Don Quixote. "I will bring the armor at once."

"But stop!" cried the innkeeper. "Have you any money?"

"Not a penny," was the answer. "I have never read of any knight carrying money with him."

"Oh, well, you are mistaken there," said the innkeeper. "The books you have read may not say anything about it. But that is because the authors never thought it worth while to write about such common things as money and clean shirts and the like."

"Have you any proof of that?"

"Most certainly I have. I know quite well that every knight had his bags stuffed full of money. Every one, also, carried some clean shirts and a small box of salve for the healing of wounds."

"It does seem reasonable," agreed Don Quixote, "but I never thought of it."

"Then let me advise you as a father advises his son," said the innkeeper. "As soon as you have been made a knight, ride homeward and provide yourself with these necessary articles."

I will obey you, most noble sir," answered Don Quixote. He then made haste and gathered his armor together. He carried it to the barnyard and laid it in a horse trough by the well.

The evening was now almost past, and it was growing dark. Don Quixote took his shield upon his left arm. He grasped his long lance in his right hand. Then he began to pace to and fro across the barnyard. He held his head high, like a soldier on duty, and would have struck fear into onlookers if the old patched helmet had not kept falling down over his face.

The full moon rose bright and clear, lighting the barnyard almost as bright as day. The innkeeper and his guests stood at the windows of the inn, and watched to see what would happen.

Presently a mule driver came into the yard to water his mules. He saw something lying in the trough, and was stooping to take it out before drawing water from the well. But at that moment Don Quixote rushed upon him.

"Stop, rash knight!" he cried. "Touch not those arms. They are the arms of the bravest man that ever lived. Touch them not, or instant death shall be your doom."

The mule driver merely grunted and paid no attention to the warning, though it would have been better for his own sake if he had listened. He grabbed the armor and threw it upon the ground.

"O my lady Dulcinea! Help me in this first trial of my valor!" cried Don Quixote.

At the same moment he lifted his lance with both hands and gave the mule driver a thrust that laid him flat in the dust of the barnyard. Another such knock would have put an end to the poor fellow. But Don Quixote was too gallant to think of striking a fallen foe.

He picked up the armor and laid it again in the horse trough. Then he went on, walking back and forth as though nothing had happened.

The poor mule driver lay senseless by the side of the trough. The innkeeper and his friends still watched from the

inn. "That mule driver is a hard-headed fellow," said one. "He is used to rough knocks, and will soon recover."

In a few minutes a noisy wagoner drove into the barnyard. He drove his team quite close to the trough. Then he began to clear it out in order to give water to his horses.

Don Quixote, however, was ready for him. He said not a word, but lifted his lance and gave the wagoner such a blow, it is a wonder that the fellow's skull was not broken.

The wagoner fell to the ground, yelling most grievously. The people in the inn were frightened, and all ran quickly to the barnyard to put an end to the rough sport.

When Don Quixote saw them coming, he braced himself on his shield and drew his sword.

"O my Dulcinea, thou queen of beauty!" he cried. "Now give strength to my arm and courage to my beating heart."

He felt brave enough to fight all the wagoners and mule drivers in the world. But just then several of the wagoner's friends came running into the barnyard, and each began to throw stones at Don Quixote.

The stones fell in a shower about his head, and he was forced to shelter himself under his shield. Yet he stood bravely at his post, and nothing could make him abandon his arms.

"Fling on!" he cried. "Do your worst. I dare you to come within my reach. Then you shall see what the reward of your folly shall be!" He spoke with such fierceness that every man shrank back in fear. Some took refuge in the barn, but kept on throwing stones.

"Let him alone," cried the innkeeper. "He is a harmless fellow who wishes to become a knight. He has lost his senses through too much reading. Come away and leave him in peace."

The men stopped throwing stones. Don Quixote put down his shield and began again to pace back and forth between the horse trough and the barn. He allowed the servants to carry away the wounded wagoner and the unconscious mule driver, but he glared at them so fiercely that they were glad to get out of his reach.

The innkeeper began to think that he had carried the sport far enough, and that it would be best to get rid of Don Quixote before any more mischief might be done. So he approached Don Quixote and said gently, "Brave sir, you have done nobly. You have guarded your armor with courage. You have shown yourself worthy of knighthood, and I will give you that honor without further delay."

"But it is not yet daybreak," answered Don Quixote. "I must guard my armor till the dawn appears."

"It is not at all necessary," said the innkeeper. "I have read of some very famous knights who stood guard only two hours. And you, sir, have watched for more than four hours, although beset by many foes."

"Time flies swiftly when one is doing his duty," said Don Quixote. "The brave man is bravest when he curbs his anger. But if I am again attacked, I shall not be able to restrain my fury. Not a man in this castle shall be left alive, unless it be to please you."

"You shall not be attacked," said the innkeeper. "Believe me, you have guarded your armor quite long enough, and I will make you a knight at once, if you are willing."

"Nothing can please me better," answered Don Quixote as he gently laid his lance down by the side of his armor.

The innkeeper then called to his guests and servants to come and see the ceremony. A book was brought to him in which he kept his accounts of hay and straw. He opened it with much dignity while Don Quixote stood with closed eyes beside his armor.

The women of the inn gathered in a circle around them. A boy held a piece of lighted candle, while the innkeeper pretended to read from the book.

The reading being finished, Don Quixote knelt down in the dust of the barnyard. The innkeeper stood over him and mumbled some words without meaning. He gave him a whack on the neck with his hand, and then slapped him on the back with the flat of his sword.

"Arise, Sir Knight," he said. "Thou art Don Quixote de la Mancha, the most valorous of men. Be brave, be brave, be always brave."

Don Quixote arose, feeling that he was now in truth a knight and ready to do valorous deeds. One of the women handed him a sword. "May your worship be a lucky knight," she said, though she had difficulty in keeping back her laughter.

Another woman arranged the green ribbons that held his helmet in place. "May you prosper, brave sir, wherever you go," she said.

Don Quixote threw his arms around the innkeeper's neck and thanked him. He could not rest until he had done some gallant deed. So he sat up all the rest of the night, polishing his armor and thinking impatiently of the morrow.

3: THE ADVENTURE WITH THE FARMER

At the earliest break of day, Don Quixote made ready to ride out in quest of adventures. He buckled on his armor. He took his lance and his shield in his hands. His gallant steed, Rocinante, stood saddled and bridled at the door of the inn.

He again embraced the innkeeper. "Farewell, thou greatest of my benefactors," he cried. "May heaven bless thee for having made me a knight." Then he mounted and sallied forth into the world. He was almost bursting with joy, for he felt that he was now in truth a knight, and his mind was filled with lofty thoughts.

Don Quixote had gone but a little way when he suddenly remembered the innkeeper's command to provide himself with money, clean shirts, and some salve for wounds.

"The command must be obeyed," he said. "I must first go home and get those necessary things."

So he turned his horse's head and took the first byroad that led towards his village. And now Rocinante seemed to have new life put into his lean body. He sniffed the air and trotted so fast that his heels seemed scarcely to touch the ground.

"This is after the manner of heroes," said Don Quixote. "Yet still I lack one thing. I need a faithful squire to ride with me and serve me. All the knights I have ever read about had squires who followed in their footsteps and looked on while they were fighting. I think, therefore, that while I am providing myself with money and shirts, I will also get me a squire."

Presently, as they were passing through a lonely place, the knight fancied that he heard cries of distress. They seemed to come from the midst of a woody thicket near the roadside.

"I thank Heaven for this lucky moment," he said to himself. "I shall now have an adventure. No doubt I shall rescue someone who is in peril, or I shall correct some grievous wrong."

He put spurs to Rocinante and rode as fast as the old horse could carry him to the spot from which the cries seemed to issue.

At the edge of the woody thicket he saw a horse tied to a small oak tree. Not far away, a lad of about fifteen years was tied to another oak. The lad's shoulders and back were bare, and it was he who was making the doleful outcry. A burly farmer was standing over him unmercifully with a horsewhip.

"Hold, discourteous knight!" cried Don Quixote, rushing up. "It is an unmanly act to strike a person who cannot strike back."

The farmer was frightened at the sudden appearance of a knight on horseback. He dropped his whip. He stood with open mouth and trembling hands, not knowing what to expect.

"Come, sir," said Don Quixote, sternly. "Take your lance, mount your horse, and we will settle this matter by a trial of arms."

The farmer answered him very humbly. "Sir Knight," he said, "this boy is my servant, and his business is to watch my sheep. But he is lazy and careless, and I have lost half of my flock through his neglect."

"What does that matter?" said Don Quixote. "You have no right to beat him, when you know he cannot beat you."

"I beat him only to make a better boy of him," answered the farmer. "He will tell you that I do it to cheat him out of his wages. But, upon my soul, he tells lies even while I am correcting him."

"Silence, base churl!" cried Don Quixote. "I say it is you who lie! I have a good mind to run you through with my lance. Untie the boy and pay him his money. Obey me this instant, and let me not hear one word of excuse from you."

The farmer, pale with fear, loosed the boy from the cord that bound him to the tree.

"Now, my young man," said Don Quixote, "how much does this fellow owe you?"

"He owes me nine months' wages at seven dollars a month," was the answer.

"Nine times seven are sixty-three," said the knight. "Sir, pay this lad what you owe him. If you wish to save your life, pay it at once."

The farmer was now more alarmed than before. He fell upon his knees. He lifted his hands, sobbed with fright, and begged for mercy.

"Noble sir," he cried, "it is too much, for I have bought him three pairs of shoes at a dollar a pair, and twice when he was sick, I paid the doctor a dollar."

"That may be," answered Don Quixote, "but we will set those dollars against the beating you have given him without cause. Come, pay him the whole amount."

"I would gladly do so," said the farmer, "but I have not a penny in my pocket. If you will let the lad go home with me, I will pay him every dollar."

At this the lad cried out, "Go home with him! Nay, not I. Why, he would beat me again and not pay me at all."

"He will not dare to do any such thing," answered Don Quixote. "I have commanded him and he must obey. Go with him, then. His money is at his house. I give him leave to go and get it. His honor as a knight will make him pay his debt to you."

"A knight!" said the lad. "He is no knight. He is only Juan Haldudo, a rich farmer."

"That may be," said Don Quixote, "but the Haldudos may have a knight in the family."

"Well, he is not much of a knight. A knight would pay his debts," said the lad.

"And he will pay you, for I have commanded him," said Don Quixote—for that, indeed, is how it always happened in the books he had read.

Then turning to the farmer he said, "Go, and make sure that you obey me. I will come this way again soon, and if you have failed, I will punish you. I will find you out, even though you hide like a lizard under a stone."

The farmer arose from his knees and was about to speak, but the knight would not listen. "I will have no words from you," he said. "You have but one task, and that is to obey. And if you would ask who it is that commands you, know that I am the valorous Don Quixote de la Mancha, the righter of wrongs and the friend of the downtrodden. And so, farewell!"

Having said this, he gave spurs to Rocinante and galloped away.

The farmer watched him until he was quite out of sight. Then he turned and called to the boy. "Come, my boy," he said. "Come to me now, and I will pay you what I owe you. I will obey this friend of the downtrodden."

"You will do well to obey him," said the boy. "He is a knight, and if you fail to pay me, he will come back and punish you."

"Oh yes, yes, I know," answered the farmer. "I will pay you everything, and more besides."

Then, without another word, he caught hold of the boy and again tied him to the tree. The boy yelled, but Don Quixote was too far away to hear his cries. The farmer fell upon him and beat him fiercely. Finally he loosed him and let him go.

"Now, boy, find your friend of the downtrodden," he said. "Tell him how well I have paid you."

The poor boy only sobbed and said nothing. He hobbled slowly away, while the farmer mounted his horse and rode grimly homeward.

In the meanwhile, Don Quixote was trotting towards his own village. He was very much pleased with himself and with his first adventure as a knight.

"O Dulcinea, most beautiful of beauties," he cried, "well mayest thou be happy. For thy knight has done a noble deed this day."

And thus he rode gallantly onward, his lance clanging against his armor at every motion of his steed.

4: THE ADVENTURE WITH THE MERCHANTS

Don Quixote had not ridden more than two miles when, at a turn in the road, he saw several horsemen approaching him.

They were merchants of Toledo, and they were going to some distant town to buy silks. There were six of them, and each carried an umbrella over his head to shield him from the sun. Following behind these horsemen were four servants and three mule drivers, all on foot.

Don Quixote's heart beat fast when he saw this company. "Here is an adventure worthy of my courage!" he cried.

He fixed himself in his stirrups, steadied his lance, and covered his breast with his shield. Then he posted himself in the middle of the road at the top of a gentle hill.

As soon as the merchants were within hearing, he cried out, "Halt there! Let all mankind stand still. No person shall pass here unless he is ready to declare that the peerless Dulcinea del Toboso is the most beautiful lady in the universe."

The merchants stopped in wonder at the strange being who thus barred their way.

"It is some poor gentleman who has lost his senses," they said to one another. Then their leader rode forward a few paces and saluted the knight.

"Sir Knight," he said, "we do not know the fair lady whom you name. If you will let us see her, and if she proves to be as beautiful as you think, we will agree to all that you require of us."

"Let you see her!" cried Don Quixote. "I might do that if I chose. But the whole point is for you to declare her the greatest beauty without seeing her"—which, of course, is how it happened in the storybooks Don Quixote had read. "Come now," he cried, "raise your right hands and say what I demand of you."

The merchants sat quietly in their saddles and made no answer.

"What!" cried Don Quixote. "Are you silent? Then know that I am your enemy, and I challenge you to combat right here and now."

He braced himself in his saddle and shook his lance, but still the merchants made no reply.

"Are you afraid, you cowards?" shouted the knight. "Come one by one, or come all together, as you please. I am ready for the combat."

Then he spurred his horse and rode furiously down the hill towards his astonished merchants. There is no telling what might have happened had Rocinante behaved himself. But that gallant steed had gone scarcely twenty yards when he stumbled and fell in the middle of the road.

Don Quixote was pitched headlong into the dust. His long lance was sent flying into the weeds on one side of the highway, while his shield landed in the bushes on the other. The knight himself rolled and tumbled on the ground, and when at last he came to rest, the weight of his rusty armor held him down.

But even as he lay helpless in the dust, he cried out, "Stay, you cowards! Do not run away. It is my horse's fault that I have been thus dismounted."

The merchants laughed. His sorry plight amused them no less than his wonderful pluck. They spread their umbrellas above their heads and rode onward over the hill.

But one of the mule drivers, who was an ill-natured fellow, picked up the fallen lance and broke it in pieces. Then with one of the longer parts he battered Don Quixote's sides until the lance was splintered into a dozen fragments. Nor did he stop until he was quite tired out.

Still Don Quixote was not conquered. Through all this storm of blows he lay daring his enemies to do their worst. "Slay me if you will," he cried, "but still I affirm that the Lady Dulcinea is without her equal on earth."

When Don Quixote found himself alone he tried once more to get on his feet. But he was unable to do so, all bruised and battered as he was.

As he lay helpless on his back it so happened that a plowman came that way. This plowman, who lived in Don Quixote's village, had been to the mill and was returning with a bag of meal on his donkey's back.

When he saw the knight sprawling in the dust, he stopped, while the donkey began to make acquaintance with poor Rocinante who was picking grass by the roadside.

"Hello, my good friend!" cried the plowman. "What has happened to you?"

Don Quixote did not answer. He looked up at the sky and began to repeat a long speech he had read in one of his books, which began something like this:

> *Where art thou, o my lady?*
> *Dost thou not grieve for my woe?*
> *Hast thou turned away, o lady,*
> *That my grief thou dost not know?*

"The fellow has lost his senses," said the plowman to himself. Then he stooped and lifted the knight's helmet from his face. It was the helmet that had been patched with pasteboard and tied on with green ribbon, but the mule driver had broken it with kicks and blows, and the ribbons were torn into shreds.

As soon as the plowman saw the knight's face he knew him. "Oh, my good neighbor Quixana!" he cried. "How came you here, and what is the matter?"

The poor gentleman paid no attention to his friend, but kept on repeating passages from his books. In fact, he was very badly hurt.

The plowman, with a good deal of trouble, lifted him up and sat him astride of the donkey. He placed him so that he could lean over and rest upon the bag of meal. Then he got all the knight's armor together, even the splinters of the lance, and tied them on the back of Rocinante.

Having seen that everything was secure, he took the steed by the bridle and the donkey by the halter, and walking before them, he made his way slowly towards the village. He trudged thoughtfully along, often looking back and speaking kindly to the wounded man. But Don Quixote, resting on the bag of meal, answered only with sighs and groans. He complained most dolefully, but would not tell how he had fallen into misfortune.

"My dear Quixana," said the plowman after a while, "I fear you do not know me."

"That is no matter," said Don Quixote. "I know who I am, and who I may be if I choose. Why, I am perhaps not only myself but a dozen other brave knights all joined in one."

It was about sunset when they reached the village. The plowman did not wish his neighbors to see the poor knight in his battered and bruised condition, for he knew that much depended upon keeping him as quiet as possible. So he tarried in a grove outside of the village until daylight had faded into dusk. Then he led the poor man to his own house.

As he went up cautiously to the door he heard voices within. The curate of the village and the barber were there. These men were neighbors of Don Quixote, and it had been their habit to come in often and spend a pleasant evening with him.

The plowman stopped at the door and listened.

"What do you think?" cried the housekeeper. "My master has not been seen for two whole days. His horse, his shield, his lance, and the old armor that was his grandfather's have also disappeared."

"Indeed! And where can he have gone?" inquired the curate.

"Where? Where but riding over the world and making believe that he is a knight!" answered the woman. "It's all because of those vile books he was forever poring over."

The niece then spoke. "Certainly it's the books," she said. "The books made him foolish. Why, I have known him to read forty-eight hours without stopping. Then he would fling the book from him and draw his sword, slashing it about him in a most fearful manner."

"I have known him to do even wilder things than that," said the housekeeper. "Once, in broad daylight, he ran around this very room shouting that he had defeated four giants as tall as church steeples. It was the books. They made him mad."

"Indeed, that's true," declared the niece. "It was the books—and they ought to be burned, every one of them."

"You are right," said the curate. "Those books have unsettled his mind. Before the setting of another sun, they should be condemned to the flames."

During all this conversation, the plowman and Don Quixote were just outside the door, unseen, in the darkening twilight. Now, without more ado, the plowman cried out,

"Hello in there! Open the gates, for here are a dozen valorous knights who bring a prisoner with them."

The housekeeper shrieked and dropped her broom on the floor. The curate and the barber rushed to the door, and the niece followed them with the lighted candle in her hand. When they saw Don Quixote astride of the donkey, they all ran to embrace him.

"Have a care," he groaned. "Be gentle, for I am sorely hurt. It was all on account of my steed failing me. Carry me to bed, and send for the enchantress Urganda to heal my wounds."

"There! Didn't I say so?" whispered the housekeeper to the curate. "His head is full of those silly books."

"Where are you wounded, uncle?" asked the niece.

"Wounded! I am not wounded. I am only bruised. I had a bad fall from Rocinante while I was fighting ten giants. You never saw such giants. They were the wickedest fellows that ever roamed the earth. But I was a match for them."

"Hear him!" whispered the curate to the housekeeper. "He talks of giants. It is as we feared. Those vile books must be condemned and burned without further delay."

They lifted the knight from the donkey's back. They helped him into the house and put him in his favorite chair. Then the women asked him a thousand questions, but his only answer was that they should give him something to eat and let him alone.

This they did. And when he had eaten a hearty supper, he crept off to bed without so much as saying goodnight.

5. THE LIBRARY

Early the next morning the curate and the barber came again. Don Quixote was still sleeping. Indeed, he did not awake until the day was more than half gone.

"We have come to remove the cause of his illness," said the curate. He asked the niece to give him the key to the room where her uncle kept his books.

"Here it is," she said, "and I hope you will make quick work of it."

They unlocked the door and went in, with the housekeeper following them. There, arranged neatly on shelves, they saw a hundred large volumes and an even greater number of smaller ones. The curate began to read the titles.

"*The Exploits of Esplandian,*" he murmured. "*The Four Books of Amadis of Gaul. The Mirror of Chivalry. The History of the Famous Knight, Tirant lo Blanch.* They are not all equally bad," he said. "Perhaps there are some that do not deserve to be burned."

"Oh, no!" cried the niece. "Do not spare any of them. Every one is bad. Every one has helped to undo my uncle."

"Throw them out of the window into the garden," said the housekeeper. "Then we will carry them around into the back yard and burn them where the smoke will not annoy anybody."

They worked all the morning. Often the curate would find a volume over which he would linger for some time. He would turn the leaves lovingly and look slyly with interest at the pictures.

"It is a great pity to burn that," he would whisper, and then he would lay the book aside for his own reading.

Most of the volumes, however, were silly and sentimental romances of knighthood and really of no value. The quick eye of the curate easily detected these, and they were cast out and doomed to destruction.

Towards noon everyone began to tire of the business. "It's no use to examine any more of these volumes," said the curate. "They're all bad. Cast them all out! Cast them out!"

The housekeeper was delighted. She kindled a bonfire in the back yard and, while the curate and the barber were resting themselves, she threw into it not only the books that had been condemned but also the pleasant volumes that the good curate had decided to spare for his own edification.

Thus the good sometimes perish with the bad.

In the afternoon Don Quixote awoke from his long sleep. He was so bruised and so lame, however, that he could not rise. He could only lie in bed and feebly mutter the names of the housekeeper and his niece.

They brought him some food, and when he had eaten it he fell asleep again.

"It is best to let him rest," whispered the curate, and they left him alone.

For two whole days the knight did not go out of his room. But he was well cared for, and though he suffered not a little, he was never heard to complain.

When Don Quixote lay helpless in his bed, the curate and the barber paid frequent visits to the house. They spent much time in stopping up the door of the little room where the knight's library had been. This they did so cunningly that the housekeeper herself could not tell exactly where the door had been.

"If he cannot find the room, he will soon forget about the books," said the curate.

On the fourth day, Don Quixote was able to walk about a little. But he did not seem to feel sure of himself or of any object about him.

The first thing he did was to look for his library. He went feebly up and down the long hallway, trying to find the door. He felt along the wall. He groped here and there, and stared confusedly around. At length he gave up the search, but he said not a word to any one.

The next day he said to the housekeeper, "I do believe that I have lost the way to the study."

"What study?" asked the woman. "There is no study in this house."

"I feel quite sure that I once had a study with many books in it," said Don Quixote.

"Oh, that was long ago," answered the housekeeper. "But during your sickness one of those wicked enchanters, about whom you have read so often, ran away with it. He took not only the room but all the books that were in it."

Don Quixote groaned.

"Yes, uncle," said the niece, "an enchanter did it. He came one night, riding on a dragon. He alighted and went into your study. In a little while he flew out through the chimney. He left the house so full of smoke that we could not see our own eyes. We looked everywhere for your library, but could find neither room nor books."

"I think I know who it was," said Don Quixote. "It was that notorious enchanter, Freston. He has a grudge against me and is my worst enemy."

"You are right, uncle," said the niece. "It was either Freston or Friston. Anyway, his name ended with *t-o-n*."

"He is the worst sort of fellow," answered the knight. "No doubt he will try to do me some other mischief. He knows where I live and will come often. But I am not afraid of him. Some day I will meet him in fair fight and vanquish him."

Then he arose and with his feeble hands took down the sword that had been hanging over the mantelpiece ever since his sad return. He felt of its edge, and murmured,

"Ah, Freston, Freston! Thou shalt yet learn of the prowess of the valorous Don Quixote de la Mancha!"

6: The Choosing of a Squire

For fifteen days the good old gentleman stayed at home. He moved quietly about the house, and seemed happy and contented. The loss of his library did not seem to disturb him.

"A true knight bears the disappointments of life with fortitude," he said.

The niece and the housekeeper, and indeed everyone else, began to hope that he would forget his strange delusions. They spoke to him cheerfully and tried to keep his mind on other things.

The curate called to see him every day, and they had many pleasant talks on many pleasant subjects. But always towards the end, Don Quixote would ramble back to the thoughts that still seemed uppermost in his memory.

"I tell you what, my dear friend," he would say. "The world would be better off if there were more knights in it. What we need most is knights, knights, plenty of knights, righting wrongs, helping the helpless, and doing great deeds for honor and glory."

Then he would go on for an hour or more talking upon his favorite subject. The good curate would nod his head and smile. He knew that it was better to humor his friend and let him have his own way.

As the days passed by, Don Quixote became more and more uneasy. The house was too quiet for him. He longed to be riding forth in quest of new adventures. He could not think or talk of anything else.

"But there is one thing lacking," he said. "I must find me a squire. All the knights that I ever read about had faithful squires who followed them on their journeys and looked on while they were fighting."

Now there lived in the village a poor man whose name was Sancho Panza. He was a laborer who had often done odd jobs about Don Quixote's farm. He was honest but poor.

To this man Don Quixote had taken a strange fancy. Almost every day he walked down the street to talk with him. He was just the kind of fellow he wished for his squire.

At last he mentioned the matter.

"Sancho Panza," he said, "I am a knight and I shall soon ride out on a knightly mission. You cannot do better than to go with me as my squire. I promise that you shall earn great renown, second only to myself."

"Renown, good master?" asked Sancho. "What sort of thing is that?"

"Why, your name will be in everybody's mouth," answered Don Quixote. "All the great ladies and gentlemen will be talking about your achievements."

"How very fine that will be!" said Sancho.

"And it may happen that in one of my adventures I shall conquer an island," continued Don Quixote. "Indeed, as I have often read, it is very likely that I shall conquer an island. Then, if you are with me, I will give it to you to be its governor."

"Well, I don't know much about islands," said Sancho, "but I'm sure I should like to govern one. So, if you'll promise me the first island you get, I'll be your man. I'll go with you and do as you say."

"I promise," said Don Quixote. "You shall be my squire. And since you will share my labors, you shall also share my rewards."

Then followed busy days for Don Quixote. He provided himself with money by selling a part of his farm. He mended his broken armor. He borrowed a lance of a friendly neighbor. He patched up his old helmet as best he could.

At last everything was in readiness, and the knight went down the street to talk with Sancho Panza. He wished to advise him of the hour he expected to start.

"I will be ready, sir," said Sancho.

"And be sure you have with you whatever it is necessary to carry," said Don Quixote.

"Indeed I will, master," said Sancho. "And I will also bring my dappled donkey along. For I am not much used to foot travel."

Don Quixote was puzzled. He could not remember reading about any knight whose squire rode on a donkey.

"Your dappled donkey? Well," he said, "you may ride him until good fortune shall present you with a horse. And I promise that the first discourteous knight who meets us shall give up his steed to you."

"I thank you, master," said Sancho Panza, "but being used to the donkey, I shall be more at home on his back than on the back of any prancing steed you might give me."

7: The Adventure with the Windmills

Very early the next morning, the knight and his squire set out on their travels. They stole silently away from the village without bidding good-bye to anyone. They made such haste that at sunrise they felt themselves quite safe from pursuit.

Don Quixote, riding in full armor, astride of gaunt Rocinante, felt that he was indeed the most valorous knight in the world. No doubt he was an impressive sight. As for Sancho Panza, he rode his little donkey, with his knapsack on one side of him and a leather bottle on the other, and his feet almost dragging the ground. His mind was full of thoughts about that island of which he hoped to be the governor.

The sun rose high above the hills. The two travelers jogged onward across the plains of Montiel. Both were silent, for both had high purposes in mind.

At length Sancho Panza spoke: "I beseech you, Sir Knight, be sure to remember the island you promised me. I dare say I shall do well enough at governing it, let it ever be so big."

Don Quixote answered with becoming dignity: "Friend Sancho, you must know that it has always been the custom of knights-errant to conquer islands and put their squires over them as governors. Now it is my intention to keep up that good custom."

"You are indeed a rare master," said Sancho Panza.

"Well, I am thinking I might even improve upon that good custom," said Don Quixote. "What if I should conquer three or four islands and set you up as master of them all?"

"You could do nothing that would please me better," answered Sancho.

While they were thus riding and talking, they came to a place where there were a great many windmills. There seemed to be thirty or forty of them scattered here and there upon the plain. When the wind blew, their long white arms seemed to wave and beckon in an almost threatening manner.

Don Quixote paused in the middle of the road. "There!" he cried. "Fortune is with us. Look yonder, Sancho! I see at least thirty huge lawless giants, and I intend to fight all of them. When I have overcome them, we will enrich ourselves with their spoils."

"What giants?" asked Sancho Panza.

"Why, those who are standing in the fields just before us," answered the knight. "See their long arms! I have read that some of these creatures have arms that reach more than two miles."

"Look at them better, master," said Sancho. "Those are not giants. They are windmills. The things you call arms are sails, and they flap around when the wind blows."

"Friend Sancho," said the knight, very sternly, "it is plain that you are not used to adventures. I tell you those things are giants. If you are afraid, go and hide yourself and say your prayers. I shall attack them at once."

Without another word he spurred Rocinante into a sturdy trot and was soon right in the midst of the windmills.

"Stand, cowards!" he cried. "Stand your ground! Do not fly from a single knight who dares you to meet him in fair fight."

At that moment the wind began to blow briskly and all the sails were set moving. They seemed to be answering his challenge.

He paused a moment. "O my Dulcinea, fairest of ladies," he cried, "help me in this perilous adventure!" Then he leveled his lance, covered himself with his shield, and rushed with Rocinante's utmost speed upon the nearest windmill.

The long lance struck into one of the whirling sails and was carried upward with such swiftness that it was torn from the knight's firm grasp. It was whirled into the air and broken into splinters. At the same moment the knight and his steed were hurled forward and thrown rolling upon the ground.

Sancho Panza hurried to the place as quickly as his dappled donkey could carry him. His master was lying helpless by the roadside. The helmet had fallen from his head, and the shield had been hurled to the farther side of the hedge.

"Mercy on me, master!" cried the squire. "Didn't I tell you they were windmills?"

"Peace, friend Sancho," answered Don Quixote, rubbing the dust from his eyes. "There is nothing so uncertain as war. That wicked enchanter, Freston, who stole my books, has done all this. They were giants, as I told you, but he changed them into windmills so that I should not have the honor of victory. But mind you, Sancho, I will get even with him in the end."

"If that is the way it is, then so be it!" cried Sancho as he dismounted from his donkey and proceeded to help his master. The faithful squire lifted the fallen knight from the ground, brought his shield, adjusted his helmet, and then led his unlucky steed to his side and helped him to remount.

With the sun sloping towards the west, knight and squire rode thoughtfully onward across the plain of Montiel.

8: THE ADVENTURE WITH THE PRISONERS

Day after day, the two travelers jogged slowly along, rambling wherever their fancy chose to wander. At length they came into the rugged highway that leads through the Black Mountains or, as they are called in Spain, the Sierra Morena.

"Now we shall have our fill of adventures," said Don Quixote.

Indeed, at the top of the first hill they saw twelve strange men trudging along the highway and slowly approaching them. The men were all in a row, one behind another. Like beads on a string, they were linked to a long chain by means of iron collars around their necks.

In front of this procession rode two horsemen with guns. At the rear marched two guards with swords and clubs.

"See there, master," said Sancho. "See those poor fellows who are being taken away to serve the king in the galleys."

"Why are they being treated so harshly?" asked Don Quixote, reining in his steed.

"Well, they are rogues," Sancho answered. "They have broken the law and been caught at it. They are now on their way to the king's galleys to be punished."

"If that is the case," said Don Quixote, "they shall have my help. For I am sworn to hinder violence and oppression."

"But these wicked wretches are not oppressed," said Sancho. "They are only getting what they deserve."

Don Quixote was not satisfied. "Still, they suffer, and they are in trouble," he answered.

Soon the chain of prisoners had come up. "Pray, sir," said Don Quixote to one of the mounted men who was captain of the guards, "why are these people led along in that cruel manner?"

"They are criminals," answered the captain. "They have been condemned to serve the king in his galleys. I have no more to say to you."

"Well, I should like to know what each one has done," said Don Quixote.

"I can't talk with you," said the captain. "But while they rest here at the top of the hill, you may ask the rogues themselves, if you wish." Then, with a sneer, he added, "They are so honest and truthful that they will not be ashamed to tell you."

Don Quixote was much pleased. He rode up and began to question the men.

"Why were you condemned to the galleys, my good fellow?" he asked of the leader.

"Oh, only for being in love," came the crafty answer.

"Indeed!" cried Don Quixote. "If all who are in love must be sent to the galleys, what will become of us?"

"True enough!" said the prisoner. "But my love was not of the common kind. I was so in love with a basket of clothes that I took it in my arms and carried it home. I was accused of stealing it, and here I am."

Don Quixote then turned to another. "And what have you done, my honest man?" he asked. "Why are you in this sad case?"

"I will tell you," answered the man. "I am here for the lack of the two gold pieces to pay an honest debt."

"Well, well, that is too bad," said the knight. "I will give you four gold pieces and set you free."

"Thank you, sir," said the prisoner. "But you might as well give money to a starving man at sea where there is nothing to buy. If I had had the gold pieces before my trial, I might now be in a different place."

Thus Don Quixote went from one prisoner to another, asking each to tell his history.

The last man in the chain was a clever, well-built fellow about thirty years old. He squinted with one eye, and had a more wicked look than any of the others. Don Quixote noticed that this man was strangely loaded with irons. He had two collars around his neck, and his wrists were so fastened to an iron bar that he could not lift his hands to his mouth.

The knight turned to one of the foot guards. "Why is this man so burdened with irons?" he asked.

"Because he is the worst of the lot," the guard answered. "He is so bold and cunning that no jail will hold him. You see how heavily ironed he is, and yet we are never sure that we have him."

"But what has he done?" asked Don Quixote.

"Done!" said the guard. "What has he not done? Why, sir, he is the famous thief and robber, Gines de Passamonte."

Then the prisoner himself spoke up quickly. "Sir, if you have anything to give us, give it quickly and ride on. I won't answer any of your questions."

"My friend," said Don Quixote, "you appear to be a man of some importance, and I should like to know your history."

"It is all written down in black and white," answered Gines. "You may buy it and read it."

"He tells you the truth," said the guard. "He has written his whole history in a book."

"What is the title of the book?" asked Don Quixote. "I must have it."

"It is called *The Life of Gines de Passamonte*, and every word of it is true," answered the prisoner. "There is no fanciful tale that compares with it for tricks and adventures."

"You are a most extraordinary man!" said Don Quixote.

By this time the guards had given the command and the human chain was again toiling slowly along over the hill. But Don Quixote was not yet satisfied. He raised himself in his stirrups and cried out, "Gentlemen of the guard, I am the renowned Don Quixote de la Mancha. I command you to release these poor men. If you refuse, then know that this lance, this sword, and this invincible arm will force you to yield."

"That's a good joke," said the captain of the guard. "Now set your basin right on top of your empty head, and go about your business. Don't meddle any more with us, for those who play with cats are likely to be scratched."

This made Don Quixote very angry. "You're a cat and a rat, and a coward to boot!" he cried. And he charged upon him so suddenly and furiously that the captain had no time to defend himself, but was tumbled headlong and helpless into the mud.

The other guards hurried to the rescue. They attacked Don Quixote with their swords and clubs. Wheeling Rocinante around, he defended himself with his heavy lance. He would have fared very badly had not the prisoners made a great hurly-burly and begun to break their chain.

Wishing to give aid to his master, Sancho leaped from his donkey, and, running up to Gines de Passamonte, began to unfasten his irons. Now all was confusion, chaos, and uproar. On one side the guards had to defend themselves from the wild thrusts of Don Quixote's lance. On the other side, they had to beat back the attacks of the prisoners, who by now had freed themselves from their irons.

In short order the guards were routed, and they fled with all speed down the highway, followed by a shower of stones from the prisoners. It was a mile to the nearest village, and there they hastened for help.

Sancho Panza remounted his donkey and drew up to his master's side. "Listen," he whispered. "The king's officers will soon be after us. Let us hurry into the forest and hide ourselves."

"Hush," said Don Quixote, impatiently. "I know what I have to do."

Then he called the prisoners around him and made a little speech: "Gentlemen, you understand what a great service I have rendered you. For this I desire no thanks or payment. But I shall require each one of you to go straightway to the city of Toboso and present himself before that fairest of all ladies, the matchless Lady Dulcinea. Give her an exact account of this famous achievement, and receive her permission to seek your various fortunes in such ways and places as you most desire."

The prisoners grinned wickedly, and Gines de Passamonte answered for them: "Most noble deliverers, that which you require of us is impossible. We must part right quickly. Some of us must skulk one way, some another. We must lie hidden in holes and among the rocks. The hounds will soon be on our tracks, and we dare not show ourselves. As to going to Toboso to see that Lady Dulcinea, why, that's all nonsense."

These words put Don Quixote into a great rage. He shook his lance at the robber, and cried out, "Now you, Sir Gines, or whatever be your name, hear me! You, yourself, shall go alone to Toboso, like a dog with a scalded tail. You shall go with the whole chain wrapped about your shoulders, and shall deliver the message as I have commanded."

In answer to this bold threat, Gines only smiled silently. But in one swift motion, his companions fell upon the knight, dragged him from his steed, and threw him upon the ground.

They stripped him of his armor and even robbed him of his long black stockings. One of them snatched the basin from his head and knocked it against a rock until it was dented and scarred most shamefully. And one broke his long lance and threw it into a thicket of thorns.

As for Sancho, he fared but little better. They took his coat, but left him his vest. They would have taken his shoes had they been worth the trouble.

Having thus amused themselves for a few hasty minutes, the rascals scattered in different directions. They were much more anxious to escape the officers of the law than to present themselves before the Lady Dulcinea del Toboso.

Thus the dappled donkey, Rocinante, Sancho Panza, and Don Quixote were left the sole masters of the field. But they were sorry masters, every one of them.

"Friend Sancho," said Don Quixote, rising from the muddy road, "there is a proverb which I desire you to remember. It is this: One might as well throw water into the sea as do a kindness to rogues."

He sought in the thicket for his broken lance, and found half of it. Then, sore and bruised, he slowly climbed upon Rocinante's back. The day was far gone, and he rode silently and thoughtfully onward into the heart of the Black Mountains. And Sancho Panza, on his dappled donkey, followed him.

9: In the Black Mountains

The darkness of night found our two travelers in the midst of the mountains and far from any friendly inn. The sky was clear, however, and above the treetops the round, full moon was shining brightly. Both knight and squire were weary from long traveling, and sore from the beating they had received from the ungrateful thieves.

At last Sancho cried, "Here we are, master!" and pulled up his donkey by the side of a huge rock. "This is a pleasant, sheltered place. Let us tarry here till morning."

"Truly, I am willing," said Don Quixote.

Both men were so tired that they were reluctant to get down from their steeds. They sat quietly in their saddles, thinking, thinking, thinking—and soon both were fast asleep.

Don Quixote sat upright, bracing himself with the remnants of the lance he had rescued from the thicket. Sancho doubled himself over upon the pommel of his saddle, and snored as peacefully as though he were on a feather bed. As for Rocinante and patient Dapple, they were no less weary than their masters. They stood motionless in their places.

It chanced about midnight that the thief, Gines de Passamonte, came to this very spot, seeking the best way to escape from the forest. As he was passing by the great rock, he was astonished to see the two beasts and their riders resting quietly in its shadow. He crept up to them very gently, not wishing to disturb their slumbers.

"Ha!" he whispered to himself, "how soundly they sleep! These two foolish fellows ride safely along the public road, and are afraid of nothing. But I, with all my cleverness, am obliged to skulk through the woods and tire myself to death with much walking. I wish I had one of these steeds."

He walked around Rocinante and gently felt his ribs and stroked his long head. "He is only a frame of bones," he said, "and there's no telling how soon he may fall to pieces. I might manage to ride him, but at the end of the road I could neither sell him nor even give him away."

Then he went softly up to the dappled donkey and examined him from his nose to his hoofs.

"This beast could carry me, and I could sell him for a dollar or two anywhere. But how shall I get him?"

He leaned against the rock and thought the matter over, while Sancho Panza made the woods echo with his snoring.

"It would be easy enough to tumble him off and take his steed by force," said Gines, still whispering to himself. "But the poor fellow did me a good turn today, and I don't like to disturb his slumbers."

Presently he took his jackknife from his pocket and went stealthily into a grove of small trees by the roadside. There, having found some slender saplings, he cut four strong poles as large as his wrist and as long as his body.

With these in his hands he returned to the donkey and slyly unbuckled the girths of the saddle. Sancho Panza, with his feet firmly in the stirrups and his short body doubled snugly upon the pommel, was not at all disturbed. He snored so loudly that no other sound could possibly be heard.

The cunning Gines smiled at his own ingenuity. He placed one end of each of his four poles under a corner of the saddle, the other end resting firmly upon the ground. Then he carefully and very gradually moved the bottom ends closer and closer to the donkey's feet. This raised the saddle some inches above the animal's back, while Sancho still slept the deep sleep of the weary.

Gines tested each pole to see that it stood like a brace, strong and secure. Then he led the donkey out from under, leaving the saddle and Sancho high up in the air.

It was a comical sight, there in the still light of the moon, and Gines de Passamonte looked back and laughed quietly. He then threw himself upon the donkey's bare back and rode joyfully away.

Sancho Panza slept and snored, and stirred not an inch. The hours of the night passed silently by as the moon and stars journeyed slowly down the western sky. At length the day dawned, and the sunlight began to peep through the trees.

Sancho was at most times an early riser. With the coming of the morning he stopped snoring. Then he slowly opened his eyes, raised his arms, and yawned. The motion of his body caused the supporting poles to twist around and give way. The saddle suddenly turned beneath him, and he fell sprawling to the ground. The sudden noise awoke Don Quixote.

"Where is thy donkey, friend Sancho?" he asked, looking quickly around.

"You may well ask where is my donkey," answered the squire, rising from the ground and rubbing his eyes. "He is gone! Some thief has led him away in the night, and left me nothing but four sticks and the saddle which I got in exchange from the barber."

"Thief, indeed!" said Don Quixote. "It was no thief. This is the work of those same wicked enchanters! They have changed the poor beast into four sticks. And now you will have to walk until we learn how to remove the enchantment and change the sticks back to a donkey."

Sancho Panza was sorely distressed. He looked at the saddle and at the sticks, and then at the tracks that the

donkey had left in the dust of the road. Tears came to his eyes, and he broke out into the saddest and most pitiful lamentation that ever was heard.

"Oh, my Dapple, my donkey, born and bred under my own roof! You were the playfellow of my children, the comfort of my wife, the envy of my neighbors. You were the easer of my burdens. And now, you are gone, gone, gone! Oh, my dear Dapple, how can I live without you?"

Don Quixote's kind heart was touched. "Never mind, dear Sancho," he said. "Dry your tears. I have five donkeys at home, and I will write an order to my niece to give you three of them. I will write it with the first pen and ink we encounter."

This generous offer turned Sancho's grief into joy. It dried his tears, hushed his cries, and changed his moans to smiles and thanks.

"You were always a good master," he said, "and I would rather meet with that pen and ink than with any number of knights."

Then knight and squire sat down together on the ground and made a paltry breakfast of some bits of dry bread. After Rocinante had eaten his fill of the sweet grass by the roadside, they resumed their journey through the mountains. Don Quixote rode in advance, and Sancho followed slowly with the donkey's saddle astride of his shoulders.

10: THE MESSAGE TO DULCINEA

One day, as Don Quixote and his squire were strolling aimlessly through the roughest part of the mountains, the knight became suddenly very silent. "Friend Sancho," he said, "as you value your life, I bid you not to speak a word to me until I give you permission."

His face wore an expression of intense concentration. He seemed to be pondering some new and weighty subject.

So, hour after hour, they toiled wearily and slowly along, and neither spoke to the other. Sancho Panza grew almost ready to burst for want of a little chat. Still, with the saddle on his shoulders, he trudged silently at the heels of Rocinante and kept his thoughts to himself.

At length, however, he could bear it no longer. He quickened his pace till he came alongside of his master. Then he laid his hand on Don Quixote's knee and spoke: "Good sir, give me your blessing, please, and let me go home to my wife and children. There I may talk till I am weary. I tell you, this tramping over hills and dales, by night and day, without opening my lips, is killing me. I cannot endure it."

"Friend Sancho, I understand," answered Don Quixote. "I give you leave to use your tongue freely so long as we are alone together on this mountain road."

"Then let us make hay while the sun shines!" cried Sancho. "I know that loose lips sink ships, but I will talk while I can, for who knows what tomorrow may bring. Every man for himself, and God for us all, say I. What's done is done, and there's no use crying over spilled milk. It's true that a closed mouth catches no flies, but easier said than done. Still, better late than never, and where there's a will there's...."

"Pray be done with your proverbs!" said Don Quixote sternly. "Now, listen to me, and I will unfold a plan I have formed for my future course, and for yours also, friend Sancho. It is my intention to send you forthwith to Toboso to carry a letter to the Lady Dulcinea. I desire that you shall start within three days. And, as you are very poor at walking, you may have the use of Rocinante, who will carry you with great safety and speed."

"Very well, master," said Sancho. "But what will you do while I am gone?"

"Do? Do you ask what I will do?" answered the knight. "Why, I have a mind to imitate that famous knight, Orlando. In proof of my devotion to my lady, I will throw away my armor, tear my clothes, pull up trees by the roots, knock my head against rocks, and do a thousand other things of that kind. You must wait and see me do some of these things, Sancho, and then you must tell the Lady Dulcinea what you have beheld with your own eyes."

"Oh, you need not go to that trouble, sir," said Sancho, "for I will tell the lady of your mad tricks just the same, and bring you back her answer full of sweet words."

"As for those 'tricks,' as you call them," said Don Quixote, "I do indeed mean to perform them quite seriously, for a knight must tell no lies."

"As it pleases you, sir," said Sancho.

"I will write the letter immediately," said Don Quixote, "and you shall set out on your journey tomorrow at sunrise."

"If you would, sir," said Sancho, "do not forget to write that order to your niece for those three donkeys that you promised me."

Using a bit of charcoal and a little notebook that he happened to find in one of his pockets, Don Quixote scrawled the letter to his lady, as well as the order for the donkeys. Sancho took the notebook and put it carefully in his coat pocket.

"Now I will mount Rocinante and be off at once," the squire announced, "for a bearer of messages should never delay his starting."

"Nay," said Don Quixote. "Wait a little, for you should see me knock my head against the rocks, and such like, before you go."

"Say not so, dear master," answered Sancho. "It would grieve me to see you playing the madman. I would cry my eyes out, and I have already blubbered too much since I lost my poor donkey."

"Then I give you leave to go," said Don Quixote.

"But tell me, good master," said Sancho, "how shall I know this out-of-the-way place when I come back? How shall I find you again in this wilderness?"

"Strew a few green branches in the path, Sancho. Strew them as you ride along till you reach the main highway. They will serve as clues to help you find your way back."

So Sancho went among the trees and cut a bundle of green boughs. Then he mounted Rocinante and prepared to take leave of his master.

"Be good to the noble steed, Sancho," said Don Quixote. "Remember to be as kind to him as you have been to his master."

"Indeed, I will not forget," said Sancho. And he rode away, strewing the boughs as he went.

11: Sancho Panza on the Road

The next day, as Sancho Panza was plodding slowly along the highway, he came to a little inn. He knew the place quite well, for he and his master had lodged there not a month before.

It was dinnertime, and the odors of the kitchen filled the air. Sancho's mouth watered at the thought of a bit of hot roast beef, for he had tasted nothing but cold victuals for many days.

He rode up and stopped outside the gate, where he enjoyed the savory smells that came to him through the open windows.

Presently, two men came out, and when they saw him at the gate, they paused. Then one said to the other, "Look there, isn't that Sancho Panza?"

"Most surely it is," said the other. "And more than that, he rides Don Quixote's horse."

Now these two men were the curate and the barber of Don Quixote's own village. They were the men who had destroyed his books, and they knew more than anyone else about the poor man's malady. They were now going through the country in search of him, for they wished to persuade him to return to the care of his family and friends. They spoke to Sancho, and he was not a little surprised to meet them in that out-of-the-way place.

"Where is your master, Sancho? Where is Don Quixote?" they asked.

"My master is engaged with some important business of his own," answered Sancho, quite stiffly.

"But where is he?" said the curate.

"That I dare not tell you," said Sancho.

"Now, Sancho Panza!" cried the barber, "don't try to put us off with any flimflam story. If you don't tell us where he is, we shall believe you have murdered him and stolen his horse. So, out with it. Tell us the truth, or we'll have you punished as you deserve."

"Oh, come now, neighbors!" said Sancho. "Why should you threaten me? I don't know where my master is at this particular moment. But I left him in yonder mountain, knocking his head against the trees, tearing up rocks, and such like."

Then he told them the whole story as I have told it to you, adding to it a great many fanciful touches of his own.

"And now," he said, "I am on my humble way to Toboso, where I mean to give a letter from my master into the hands of the Lady Dulcinea."

"Let us see the letter," said the barber.

Sancho put his hand into his pocket to get the notebook. He fumbled a great while without finding it. He searched first in one pocket, then in another. He searched in his sleeve and in his hat. But had he searched forever, he would not have found it. It had slipped through a hole in his pocket and was lost in the dust of the highway.

He turned pale, and his hands trembled. Then he began to rave and to stamp like a madman. He tore his beard. He beat himself with his fists.

"Why need you be so angry, Sancho?" asked the curate, kindly. "What is the matter?"

"Oh," he cried, "I deserve the worst beating in the world, for I have lost three donkeys which were as good as three castles."

"How so?" asked the barber. "Were the donkeys in your pocket?"

"Not exactly," answered Sancho. "But I have lost the notebook that contained not only the letter to Dulcinea, but an order to Don Quixote's niece for three of his five donkeys."

Then with tears and sobs, the poor man told them how he had recently lost his own Dapple, the joy of his household, the hope of his life.

"Cheer up, Sancho," said the curate. "We are going to find your master, and I will see that he gives you another written order in proper form."

"Will you indeed?" said Sancho, brightening up. "Well then, the loss is not so bad after all. As for Dulcinea's letter, I don't care a straw about that. I know it all by heart, and will carry it to her by word of mouth. In other words, I will repeat it to her, just as it was written. And I will repeat it to you, if you wish."

"You speak like a wise man," said the curate. "But what concerns us now is to find your master and persuade him to give up his mad pranks and projects. So, come into the inn with us, and we'll talk it over while we eat dinner."

"You two may go in," answered Sancho, "but as for me, I feel best out here in the open air. However, you may send me a dish of hot victuals, if you like, and I'll eat while I'm waiting. And you may tell the stable boy to bring Rocinante an armful of fodder."

So Sancho sat at the gate while the curate and the barber went inside. Presently a dish of hot meat was sent out to him, and he feasted as he had not feasted for many a day.

The hearty meal put him in fine humor. And, as he thought over the words of the curate and the barber, he made up his mind to return with them into the mountains. He was anxious to receive from Don Quixote a second order for the three donkeys.

He had scarcely finished his meal when the curate and the barber came riding out, ready to begin the journey, and wearing disguises to conceal their true identities from Don Quixote. They wasted no time on their journey, and late that very afternoon they reached the place where Sancho had strewn the green branches in the road.

"It was right about here that I left him," he said.

And sure enough, they soon discovered the knight sitting quietly upon a rock and gazing at the sky. He was pale and almost starved, and Sancho could hear him sighing dolefully and muttering the name of the Lady Dulcinea.

I need not stop here to tell of the manner in which Don Quixote received his friends, who were so disguised that he did not know them. Nor shall I describe the ingenious trick by which they convinced him to put on his armor again and ride with them out of the forest.

At first, all went well, for the knight was persuaded that he was going to the aid of a fair princess whom a tyrant had driven from her kingdom.

"Come!" he cried, as he mounted Rocinante. "Let us all go together and avenge the wrongs of this unfortunate lady."

As they set out, Sancho was obliged to travel on foot again, while the rest rode along the highway on horseback. But the squire's heart was light and free, and he kept thinking of the three donkeys and the glorious time when Don Quixote would make him the governor of an island.

The next day, when the party was well out of the mountains, they saw a stranger riding slowly along at a little distance ahead. He was dressed like a gypsy, and was mounted upon a small donkey that he could not by any means urge out of a snail's pace.

Sancho Panza's eyes opened very wide. For at the first glance he knew that the gypsy was none other than the thief, Gines de Passamonte, and that the donkey was his own long-lost Dapple.

The next moment he was running to overtake the pair. And although Gines tried hard to whip the donkey into a trot, Sancho was soon beside them.

"Ah, you thief!" he shouted. "Get off from the back of my dear beast. Away from my Dapple! Away from my comfort! Take to your heels and be gone."

He had no need to use so many words. For Gines, seeing several men so close upon him, dismounted quickly and took to his heels. No doubt he thought that the king's officers were after him, for he bounded into the woods, and was soon out of sight.

And now Sancho's joy was too great to be described. He stroked the donkey with his hands, he kissed it again and again, and he called it by every endearing name.

"My treasure, my darling, my dear Dapple! Is it possible that I have you again? How have you been since I last saw you?" he cried.

As for the donkey, it was as silent as any donkey could be. It said not one word in answer to Sancho's questions, but allowed him to kiss its nose as often as he pleased.

The rest of the company rejoiced at the squire's good fortune, and Don Quixote said, "I am glad that you have found your beast, Sancho. But it shall make no difference with the order I have written to my niece. She is to give you the three donkeys, just the same."

"I thank you, sir," said Sancho. "You were always a kind master."

12: WITH FRIENDS AND NEIGHBORS

For nearly a month Don Quixote remained at home, seeing no one at all but his niece and the housekeeper. The curate and the barber came daily to ask how he was doing, but they kept carefully out of his sight. "We do not wish to excite him," they said, "for that might hinder his recovery."

At length the niece told them that he was well and in his right mind. Would they not come in and see him?

"With much pleasure," answered the barber, and they were ushered in.

They found the poor gentleman sitting up in his bed, with a red nightcap on his head. His eyes were bright, and his voice was clear, but his face and body were so withered and wasted that he looked like a mummy.

He seemed glad to see his two old friends. They sat down by his bedside and talked with him about a great many matters. They tried to say nothing about knights and their adventures, but at last the subject came up in spite of them.

Then Don Quixote grew eloquent. He talked about knights and giants and famous heroes, scarcely giving the curate room to put in a word.

His friends saw with sadness that his mind still ran towards the same great passion. They saw that it was his intention, sooner or later, to ride out again to seek new adventures. So, when at last they took their departure, the curate again whispered a word of caution to the niece.

"Keep a good watch upon him," he said. "Let everything be very quiet around him, and don't let him think about going away from home."

As Don Quixote improved in strength and became able to walk about the house, other neighbors and friends dropped in to see him. He welcomed each one cheerfully, and never failed to say something in praise of knighthood. But they, having been cautioned by the curate, talked to him only about the weather and the crops, and soon took their leave. And so the poor man gradually grew stronger and seemed to be quite well contented.

One morning, however, who should knock at the door but Sancho Panza.

"I have come to see the valorous Don Quixote," he said to the niece.

"You shall see nobody!" she answered, holding the door against him. "You shall not enter this house, you vagabond!"

"Go, go!" cried the housekeeper. "All along it was you and no one else who enticed him to go a-rambling all over the world."

"No such thing," answered Sancho. "It's I that have been enticed and carried a-rambling, and not your master. It was he that took me from house and home, saying he would give me an island, and I'm still waiting for it."

"An island! What's that?" said the niece. "If it's anything to eat, I hope it'll choke you."

"You're wrong there," answered Sancho. "Islands are not to eat; they're to govern."

"Well, anyhow, you don't come in here," said the niece. "Go govern your own house, plow your own field, and don't trouble yourself about anybody's islands."

It so happened that the curate and the barber, who were just taking their leave after a short visit, heard the whole of this little quarrel. They were much amused by it, and were about to give their help to the niece when Don Quixote himself came to the door.

"Welcome, my faithful friend," he said. And, giving his niece a sharp rebuke, he led Sancho into the house.

"Now mark me," whispered the curate, "our neighbor will soon be rambling again in spite of all that we can do."

Don Quixote led his squire into the bedroom and locked the door. Then the two sat down together and talked of the glories and perils of knighthood.

"What say you, friend Sancho?" said the knight. "Will you return to my service? What does your good wife say?"

"She says," answered Sancho, "that a bird in the hand is worth two in the bush, and that one hold-fast is better than two may-be-so's. She says, better safe than sorry, and look before you leap. She says…."

"Yes, yes," said Don Quixote, "indeed, you talk like pearls today. But what shall I understand from all that?"

"Why, sir," answered Sancho, "to come to the point, I wish you to give me so much a month for my wages. For other rewards come late, and may not come at all. And a little in one's own pocket is better than much in another's purse."

"Friend Sancho," said Don Quixote, "I understand the drift of all your proverbs."

"Certainly," answered Sancho, "and I should like to know what I am going to get. If you should sometime give me that island, I would then be willing to knock a proper amount off of the wages."

"As to the wages," said Don Quixote, "I would pay them willingly if it were allowed by our order. But in all the books I have ever read, there is no account of a knight paying wages to his squire. The servant was always given an island, or something of that sort and there was an end of it."

"But suppose that the island was not forthcoming?" said Sancho.

"I must abide by the customs of chivalry," said Don Quixote firmly. "If you desire not to take the same risks of fortune as myself, heaven be with you. I can find a squire more obedient and careful than you have ever been, and much less talkative."

Sancho's heart sank within him. He had not expected an answer like this. In fact he had thought that Don Quixote could not possibly do without him. He was so taken aback that he did not know what to say or do.

At that moment there was a knock at the door. In came the housekeeper and the niece, and with them a young man of the village whose name was Samson Carrasco. He was a neighbor, now twenty-four years old and just home from the great college at Salamanca. He had a round face, a large mouth, and eyes that sparkled with good humor.

"You are a scholar," whispered the niece, as they entered the room. "He may listen to you, a man of learning. Please, try to persuade him from riding out again."

Samson Carrasco was indeed a man of learning, but he was also an actor and a mimic, and he liked nothing so much as a good joke. He could not resist playing a role as he threw himself at Don Quixote's feet and delivered this flattering speech:

"Oh flower of chivalry," he cried, "shining glory of arms, the pride of Spain! Let all who would prevent you from sallying forth yet again be disappointed in their ungenerous wishes."

Then, turning to the housekeeper, he said, "You must not detain him, for while he stays here idle, the poor are without a helper, orphans are without a friend, the oppressed are without a defender, and the world is deprived of a most valorous knight."

To this speech the housekeeper could only gape in reply, and Samson therefore turned again to Don Quixote.

"Go forth, then, my graceful, my fearless hero," he said. "Let your greatness shine. And if you need anything for your comfort or your service, I am here to supply it. I am ready to do anything. I am ready, yes, eager, to attend you as your squire and faithful servant."

Don Quixote was deeply moved. He took the young man by the hand and said, "No, my friend. It would be unfair that Samson Carrasco, the glory of the Salamanca schools, should devote his talents to such a purpose. Remain in thy country, for the honor of Spain and the delight of thy parents. Although Sancho declines to go with me, there are plenty of others who will be glad to serve as my squire."

At these words Sancho burst into tears and cried out, "Oh, I'll go, I'll go! I have not a heart of flint, dear master. If I spoke about wages, it was only to please my wife."

So the two embraced, and were as good friends as before. And, with the advice of Samson Carrasco, it was agreed that on the third day they would set out on their new adventures.

The niece and the housekeeper made a woeful outcry. They scolded, they pleaded, and they wept bitter tears. But nothing could change the designs of the valorous knight.

The curate and the barber, as well as the women, blamed Samson Carrasco for the whole business. But he understood the case better than they. "It is wiser not to restrain him," he said. "He will find the cure for his malady not here, but on the road. So for the moment, let us humor him."

Towards evening on the appointed day, Don Quixote mounted his Rocinante, and Sancho threw himself astride of his faithful Dapple. The knight carried a new lance and wore a new helmet of brass that his friend Samson had given him. The squire carried a knapsack well filled with provisions and a purse stuffed with money for any expenses.

The niece and the housekeeper stood at the door, waving their good-byes, and Sancho's wife, watching from her window, wept her farewells as they passed. Samson Carrasco walked with them to the edge of the village, and there bade them farewell.

And so, knight and squire rode forth with solemn faces and high-minded purposes, ready to encounter whatever fate was in store for them.

"Friend Sancho," said Don Quixote, "our first duty is plain. Before undertaking any feat of arms we must make our way to the city of Toboso, and there perform those acts of homage due to the peerless Lady Dulcinea."

"It is even as you command, Sir Knight," answered Sancho.

Therefore, to Toboso they made their way.

In the afternoon of the second day they came in sight of that notable place. Since Don Quixote did not know the house in which Dulcinea lived, he thought it best to tarry outside until after nightfall. They therefore spent the evening under some oaks a little way from the road, and did not enter Toboso until about midnight.

As they rode along the grass-grown street, the whole world seemed silent. There was no one stirring in the city.

The people were all asleep. There was no light except that of the moon. The heart of Don Quixote was filled with forebodings.

"My dear Sancho," he whispered hoarsely, "show me the way to her palace."

"Palace!" said Sancho. "What palace do you mean? When I saw her, she was living in a small cottage."

Now, in truth, he had never seen her at all, but he wished to make believe that he had seen her when his master had sent him with the letter.

They rode slowly along the street until they approached a large building, which loomed tall and dark in the dim moonlight.

"This must be it," said Don Quixote. "Here is my Dulcinea's palace, and it is well worthy of the exquisite lady." But when he rode closer, he discovered that it was no palace at all, but only the great church of the town.

"We have made a mistake, Sancho," he said. "This is not her dwelling place, and we shall have to look farther."

They rode onward to the end of the street. Then they came back and looked through every byway and alley, but they could not find anything that looked like a palace.

The night began to wear away. A faint light appeared in the east. It grew larger and brighter, and soon overspread the sky. The swallows that were nesting under the eaves began to twitter. Morning was nigh at hand.

Here and there a door opened, and the sound of voices broke the stillness of the town. The people were beginning to stir.

As knight and squire paused in the street, uncertain what to do, a young countryman came along, driving a pair of mules and singing a song. "Good morning, honest friend," said Don Quixote. "Pray tell me, where is the palace of the peerless princess, the Lady Dulcinea del Toboso?"

"Sir," answered the young fellow, "I've just lately come to Toboso, and, to be sure, I don't know of any princesses or palaces in this of all places."

Having said this, he switched his mules and drove on, singing louder than before.

It was now broad daylight. The sun was almost above the trees. There would soon be other passers-by in the street. Sancho Panza began to feel uneasy.

"I think, sir," said he, "that it would not be good for us to sit here and be stared at by everybody in the town. We had better slip out to some grove not far away. Then while you lie there hidden, I will come back and search every hole and corner for the Lady Dulcinea. When I find her, I'll talk to her and tell her that you are close by, waiting for her orders. This, of course, will make her all the more ready to receive you."

"Dear Sancho," answered Don Quixote, "you were always wise. You have said a thousand sentences in a few words, and I will do exactly as you say."

Without further loss of time, therefore, they turned their steeds about and rode out of town to a grove some two miles away. There Don Quixote concealed himself among the trees, bidding Sancho Panza return and make haste to discover the whereabouts of the Lady Dulcinea.

"Cheer up, master!" Sancho replied as he rode away. "I'll be back here in a jiffy. Faint heart never won fair lady."

"Sancho," said the knight, "you have a rare talent for quoting proverbs." But the squire was already riding briskly away towards the town.

He did not ride far. At the foot of a little hill he paused and looked back. Seeing that he was out of his master's sight, he stopped under a tree by the roadside, and began to talk with himself.

"Friend Sancho, where are you going? Are you hunting for a mule?"

"No, not for any mule."

"What, then, are you doing?"

"I am looking for a princess who is the sum of all beauty."

"Where do you think you will find her?"

"Where? Why, in the great city of Toboso. But it's like looking for a needle in a haystack."

"Why then do you undertake such a thing?"

"Why? To please my master, of course. But if he is mad enough to mistake windmills for giants, it will not be hard to make him believe that any country girl is the Lady Dulcinea."

"Certainly, it will not."

"Well, that is just what I'll do. It will be the easiest way out of this troublesome business."

So, having finished this conversation with himself, he dismounted and sat down under a tree. The shade was pleasant, and he remembered the provisions he had in his knapsack. When he had eaten a hearty breakfast, he lay down and slept until it was far past midday.

At last he awoke feeling rested and contented. "This is better than riding through Toboso, hunting for Dulcinea's palace," he said.

He had just remounted his donkey when, looking down the road, he saw three country girls coming up from the town. They were awkward and red-faced, and were riding slowly along on donkeys.

Sancho did not wait a moment, but turned his steed quickly about and made all haste back to his master.

"Well, my good Sancho, what news?" asked the knight eagerly.

"Oh, the best of news, sir!" answered Sancho. "The Lady Dulcinea with her two maids is coming out to meet you. She is close at hand even now. So, mount Rocinante quickly, and get into the road where you can see her for yourself and greet her in a becoming manner."

"I can hardly believe such news, Sancho," said Don Quixote. "Do not add to my grief by deceiving me."

"Deceive you, sir? Why should I wish to play a trick on you? Come, ride out with me quickly, and you will see the princess coming. She and her damsels sparkle with gold, pearls, diamonds, and rubies. There was never so much beauty seen in Spain."

"Let us hasten then, Sancho," said Don Quixote, climbing upon Rocinante with uncommon speed. "And I promise to reward you for your good news. You shall have the best spoils of our next adventure. And if that is not enough, I will give you the three colts I have at home."

"I shall be very glad to get the colts, master, and I thank you," said Sancho, "but as for spoils, I'm not particular."

They rode hastily out of the grove and were soon on the highroad at the crest of the hill. Looking down towards the town, they could see no one but the three country lasses approaching slowly on their donkeys.

Don Quixote's face showed his deep disappointment. He paused and looked backward and forward, this way and that.

"I don't see her, Sancho," he said. "Are you sure that she has left the city?"

"Why, where are your eyes, master?" answered the squire. "Don't you see her right here with her two lovely maidens?"

"I see nothing but three country girls on three very scrawny donkeys."

"Well! Is it possible that you mistake the princess for an awkward country girl? Can't you tell a beautiful palfrey from a miserable donkey?"

"To tell you the truth, Sancho, I see nothing but three donkeys carrying three red-faced country girls. They are coming towards us, and I see them quite plainly. But where is the princess?"

"Oh, master, master! How blind you are! There is no country girl in sight. It is the princess whom you see, and she is drawing nearer every moment. Let us hasten and speak to her."

So saying, Sancho spurred his donkey onward, and hurried down the hill to meet the girls. He leaped to the ground in the middle of the road before them. He placed himself in front of the most awkward of the three. He lifted his hat and fell upon his knees.

"Queen and princess of beauty, listen to my prayer," he began. "If it please your highness and haughtiness, grant to take into your liking yonder knight who is your humble captive. I am Sancho Panza, his famous squire, and he is the wandering champion, Don Quixote de la Mancha."

By this time Don Quixote had also dismounted and was kneeling in the middle of the road. It was hard for him to believe that this homely damsel was his queen, the Lady Dulcinea, for she was coarse in form and manners. Yet he tried to imagine that some enchanter had changed her into this form.

"Get out of our way!" screamed the angry girls. "We're in a hurry to get home."

But Sancho knelt unmoved in the very pathway of their mules. "Oh, universal lady," he said, "does not your heart melt in pity? See there, how the post and pillar of knighthood is offering his homage to you."

"Listen to his gibberish!" cried one of the girls. "Get out of the way!"

With that, they urged their donkeys forward and crowded past. The next moment they were speeding away in a cloud of dust and were soon at the top of the hill.

Don Quixote rose from the ground and looked after them. He watched them with sorrowful eyes until a turn in the road hid them from sight. Then he turned to the squire, and said with a deep sigh, "Sancho, what do you think of this business? Aren't those enchanters the most evil-minded creatures you ever saw? They were not content with turning my Dulcinea into the likeness of a coarse country girl. Why, they even went so far as to take from her the sweet, flowery perfume that hangs about her like a morning mist. For didn't you notice that strong whiff of raw onions as she passed us? It almost took my breath away."

"Oh, those enchanters!" cried Sancho. "They don't stop at any kind of wickedness. I wish I could see them all strung on a thread and hung up to dry, like a lot of herrings."

"Ah well, ah well!" sighed Don Quixote. "I have said it before, and I will say it a thousand times: I am the most unlucky man in the universe." Then he remounted Rocinante, and rode on, very sad and silent. He rode on through the town and down the long, dusty highway, not caring whither he went. And Sancho Panza followed him.

14: THE KNIGHT OF THE WHITE MOON

One morning, Don Quixote, fully armed, rode out to the seashore to take the air. On this day he felt very brave, and was in fine fighting humor.

"A strong suit of armor," he said, "is my best attire, and combat is my meat and drink."

Suddenly he saw a strange knight riding towards him. The knight was armed from head to foot, and on his shield a bright moon was painted.

As soon as he was within hearing, he called out, "Most illustrious, most valorous Don Quixote de la Mancha, I am the Knight of the White Moon. I have come to enter into combat with you. I have come to make you confess that my lady, whoever she may be, is more beautiful by far than thy Dulcinea del Toboso."

"That I will never confess," answered Don Quixote, "but I will force you to confess the contrary. Thou hast never seen the illustrious Dulcinea. If thou hadst, the sight of her would have made you know that there is no beauty like unto hers."

"I challenge you to prove it in fair combat," cried the Knight of the White Moon. "If I vanquish you, I shall require you to go to your home, and for the space of one year give up your arms and live there in peace and quiet."

"But what do you agree to do if I vanquish you?" said Don Quixote.

"Then you may do with me what you will," answered the knight. "My horse and arms shall be your spoils, and the fame of my deeds shall be added to that of your own achievements."

"I accept your challenge," said Don Quixote, "and will faithfully comply with all its conditions. But I am content with the fame of my own deeds, and do not wish to assume yours. Choose whichever side of the field you prefer, and let us settle this business at once."

The two knights turned their horses and rode apart some distance. Then they again faced each other. The next moment, without waiting for any signal, they charged.

The White Moon's steed was much swifter than Rocinante, and he thundered down upon Don Quixote. Our knight had no time to use his spear. The stranger struck him with such force that both he and his steed were hurled helpless to the ground.

Quickly the Knight of the White Moon dismounted. He held his spear at Don Quixote's throat and cried, "Yield, knight! Fulfill the conditions of our challenge or your life is forfeit!"

Bruised and stunned, Don Quixote answered in a faint and feeble voice, "I maintain that Dulcinea del Toboso is the most beautiful lady in the world, and I am the most unfortunate knight. Press on thy spear, and rid me of life."

"That I will not do," said he of the White Moon. "I will not dispute the fame of the beautiful Dulcinea. I shall be satisfied if the great Don Quixote will only return to his home for a year as was agreed to in our challenge."

"Very well," answered Don Quixote. "Since you require nothing that will tarnish the fame of the Lady Dulcinea, I will do all the rest as you desire."

He lifted Don Quixote from the ground and uncovered his face. The poor old knight was very pale and weak.

When Sancho Panza rode forth to aid his master, he was so sad and dismayed that he did not know what to do.

The Knight of the White Moon galloped away towards the city, and some of those who had seen the combat followed him. They asked him who he was, and why he had dealt so roughly with the famous but harmless Don Quixote.

"My name is Samson Carrasco," said the knight, "and I am a friend and near neighbor of Don Quixote. All that I wished in this combat was not to harm my friend, but to make him promise to return home. I think that if he can be brought to rest there quietly for a year, all this madness about knights and adventures will be cured."

15: THE LAST ADVENTURE OF ALL

For six days Don Quixote lay in bed in a nearby inn, sullen and sorrowful. All this time Sancho Panza sat beside him and tried to comfort him.

"My master," he said, "pluck up your head and be of good cheer if you can. Let us go home and quit seeking adventures in lands and places we do not know. And," concluded Sancho, as he thought of the island he would never govern, "if you will only think, I am the one who loses most, though it is you who are in the worst pickle."

The squire's cheerful words gave fresh hope to the knight. Gradually his courage came back to him, and at length the two started for home. Don Quixote rode on Rocinante. He was unarmed and clad in a traveling coat. Sancho followed him leading his donkey, which was laden with Don Quixote's armor.

They traveled for many days with their faces turned steadfastly towards La Mancha. They made slow progress, and they stopped often by the way.

At length they got to the top of a hill from which they could see their own peaceful little village lying in the green valley below. At this sight Sancho fell upon his knees and cried out, "Oh, you long-wished-for village, open your eyes and behold your child, Sancho Panza. He has come back to you again, with no more riches but with plenty of bruises for his troubles. Oh village, open your arms and receive also your son, Don Quixote. While he has been vanquished by others, he has gained the victory over himself—and that is the best of all victories."

"Hush," said Don Quixote, "and let us put our best foot forward to enter our village."

So they went down the hill, and were soon met by their old friends, the curate, the barber, and faithful Samson Carrasco. Don Quixote alighted and embraced them all quite lovingly.

"I have returned home for a year," he said. "I have a plan to turn shepherd and enjoy the solitude of the fields. If you have not much to do, I shall be pleased to have you for my companions."

They answered him pleasantly, and then made their way to Don Quixote's house. The housekeeper and the niece were at the door to welcome the wanderer.

"My dear niece," he said, "I have come home for a little while. I think that I shall soon leave you again, to live the simple life of a shepherd. But for now, help me to bed, for it seems to me that I am not very well."

They led him in and made him as comfortable as they could. They cared most lovingly for him day and night. But all the strength seemed to have gone from his poor body.

The curate, the barber, and Samson Carrasco came often to see him. His good squire, Sancho Panza, sat all the time by his bedside. But in spite of every care he steadily grew weaker.

On the sixth day the doctor told him that he was in danger and might not live long. Don Quixote asked them to leave him alone for a little while, for he thought that he could sleep.

They went out of the room. He soon fell into a deep slumber, and he lay so still, with such a look of peace upon his face, that they thought he would never wake in this world.

At the end of six hours, however, he opened his eyes, and said, "Send for my good friends, the curate and the barber and Samson Carrasco, for I am at death's door, and I wish to make my will."

But these gentlemen had all the time been waiting at the door, and now they entered the room. Don Quixote was overjoyed to see them. "Welcome, kind friends!" he said. "I am no longer Don Quixote de la Mancha, but plain Alonzo Quixana. My mind is clear now, and I see the great folly that I was led into through the reading of foolish books. All those stories of knights and magicians are hateful to me, and I abhor them. But now send for my lawyer, that he may draw up my will, for my hours are numbered."

They looked at one another in wonder, until Samson Carrasco roused himself to go and fetch the lawyer.

The man of law came and sat down by his bedside, and the will was drawn up in proper form. It provided that a sum of money should be paid to Sancho Panza for his good services, and that the rest of the estate should go to the niece. It was signed by Alonzo Quixana, and witnessed by the curate and the barber.

Then the sick man fell back in his bed and lay for three days without knowing anything at all. In the afternoon of the third day he fell into a gentle sleep from which he never awoke.

So ended the adventures of as good and true a man as Spain has ever known.